Dear ....

MERRY CHRISTMAS

With love from

....

First published in hardback in 2013 by Hodder Children's Books
This paperback edition published in 2014.

Illustration copyright © Zdenko Basic and Manuel Šumberac 2013

Hodder Children's Books, 338 Euston Road, London, NW1 3BH
Hodder Children's Books Australia, Level 17/207 Kent Street,
Sydney, NSW 2000

A catalogue record of this book is available from the British Library.

ISBN: 978 1 444 9 0243 3

Printed in China

Hodder Children's Books is a division
of Hachette Children's Books,
an Hachette UK Company

www.hachette.co.uk

The Night Before Christmas

Written by Clement C. Moore

Illustrated by Zdenko Basic and Manuel Šumberac

A division of Hachette Children's Books

'TWAS THE NIGHT BEFORE CHRISTMAS,

WHEN ALL THROUGH THE HOUSE

Not a creature was stirring, not even a mouse.

The stockings were hung by the chimney with care,

In hopes that Saint Nicholas soon would be there.

The children were nestled all snug in their beds,
While visions of sugarplums danced in their heads.
And Mama in her kerchief and I in my cap
Had just settled down for a long winter's nap.

When out on the lawn there arose such a clatter,
I sprang from my bed to see what was the matter.
Away to the window I flew like a flash,
Tore open the shutters and threw up the sash.

NORTH POLE
25 DEC

The moon on the breast of the new-fallen snow
Gave the lustre of midday to objects below,
When what to my wondering eyes should appear,
But a miniature sleigh and eight tiny reindeer,
With a little old driver so lively and quick,
I knew in a moment it must be Saint Nick!

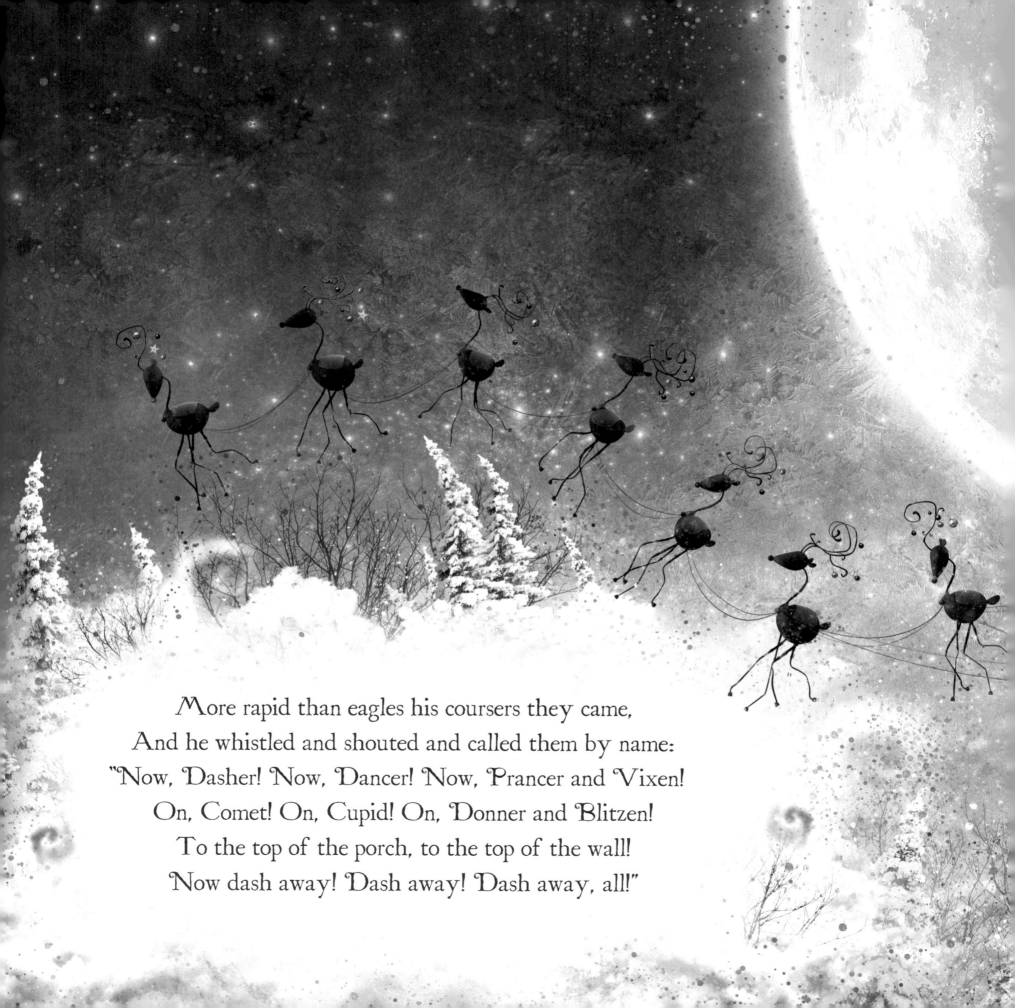

More rapid than eagles his coursers they came,
And he whistled and shouted and called them by name:
"Now, Dasher! Now, Dancer! Now, Prancer and Vixen!
On, Comet! On, Cupid! On, Donner and Blitzen!
To the top of the porch, to the top of the wall!
Now dash away! Dash away! Dash away, all!"

As dry leaves that before the wild hurricane fly,
When they meet with an obstacle, mount to the sky,
So up to the housetop the coursers they flew,
With sleigh full of toys and Saint Nicholas, too.
And then, in a twinkling, I heard on the roof
The prancing and pawing of each little hoof.

He was dressed
all in fur from
his head to his foot,
And his clothes were
all tarnished with
ashes and soot.

As I drew in
my head and
was turning around,
Down the chimney
Saint Nicholas
came with a bound.

A bundle of toys he had flung on his back,
And he looked like a peddler just opening his pack.
His eyes how they twinkled! His dimples how merry!
His cheeks were like roses, his nose like a cherry!

His droll little mouth was drawn up like a bow,
And the beard on his chin was as white as the snow.
The stump of a pipe he held tight in his teeth,
And the smoke, it encircled his head like a wreath.

He had a broad face and a little round belly
That shook when he laughed like a bowl full of jelly.
He was chubby and plump, a right jolly old elf,

And I laughed when I saw him, in spite of myself.
A wink of his eye and a twist of his head
Soon gave me to know I had nothing to dread.

He spoke not a word, but went straight to his work,
And filled all the stockings, then turned with a jerk,

And laying his finger aside of his nose,
And giving a nod, up the chimney he rose.

He sprang to his sleigh, to his team gave a whistle,
And away they all flew like the down of a thistle.

But I heard him exclaim ere he drove out of sight,
"Happy Christmas to all,
and to all a Good Night!"

Look out for these other winter classics:

THE
NATIVITY PLAY
Nick Butterworth and Mick Inkpen
978 0 340 39894 4

Miki
Stephen Mackey
978 0 340 95065 4

THE TOOTH FAIRY'S
CHRISTMAS
PETER BENTLY GARRY PARSONS
978 1 444 91834 2

Stephen Mackey
Miki
and the Wishing Star
978 1 444 90137 5

25 years of Kipper
Kipper's
Christmas Eve
Mick Inkpen
978 1 444 91623 2

Tickly Christmas
Wibbly Pig!
Mick Inkpen
As seen on TV
978 0 340 99753 6

For fun activities, further information and to order, visit www.hodderchildrens.co.uk